Voices in My Head

Addison Ferry

ISBN 979-8-89130-677-6 (paperback)
ISBN 979-8-89130-678-3 (digital)

Christian Faith Publishing
832 Park Avenue
Meadville, PA 16335
www.christianfaithpublishing.com

Printed in the United States of America

Dedication

To my parents and family for always supporting me in everything I do! Also to Lynn Cook for inspiring me!

Chapter 1

"Wake up! Something's wrong!"

"What is it?"

"I don't know, but there's something terribly wrong!"

"What is going on? I'm getting worried!"

"Ali, you can't breathe!"

"I am breathing right now!"

"You aren't breathing!"

"Yes, I am! Shut up!"

"You can't breathe! You are suffocating, and you are going to die! Ali, you are going to die!"

"I can't breathe! Why am I shaking? I can't feel my hands! Where am I? What is going on?"

*****

I am jerked from my sleep, and I jolt up.

"Maddix!" I scream. My brother Maddix rushes into my room.

"What is it, Ali?" Maddix asks worriedly.

"It's happening again. I don't know why!" I stutter. Maddix doesn't say a word. He grabs my weighted blanket and the glass of water I keep beside my bed. He sits next to me and rubs my head.

"Think of all the beautiful things surrounding you. What do you see?"

"I see my door, a chair, clothes, trash." I sob.

"All right, what can you feel?"

"Your hand rubbing my head."

"What can you smell?"

"Lavender from my Scentsy," I say calmly. Maddix rubs my head until I finally fall asleep. He is the best brother a girl could ask for.

I don't quite remember when the voice first started; it has been around for as long as I can remember. I don't know its name. I don't know its gender. I just know it scares me. I've tried to imagine what it would look like. I have drawn many pictures of it, but none of them seem to be suitable. I have only told Maddix about the voice because he hears one too. I haven't told anyone else because it is hard to explain it to others, especially if they have never experienced it. Sometimes, my voice can be obnoxious, while other times, it is chill. However, it is always with me wherever I go—kind of like a dog with its owner.

The sun beams through my window, calling me to wake up. Instead, I throw my blanket over my head, but I am not allowed to stay there long because Maddix storms into my room.

"Rise and shine, loser! You have ten minutes to get ready! Last day of school!" He sings.

I ignore him and stay hidden from the light. However, Maddix is not amused and proceeds to drag me out of bed. I groan loudly and kick my legs in an attempt to fight back. We both know who is going to win this fight, but I never make it easy. I finally give in and start to get dressed for school. I know Daddy has already left for work. He is never home when we wake up, and Momma is preparing breakfast for Maddix and me.

I am not a morning person. I never have been, and I never plan to be. I throw my long hair into a messy bun and throw on a pair of joggers, along with a hoodie. After last night, I have no ambition to look presentable today. I am hoping I can just blend into the crowd at school. I usually do; not many people talk to me unless I'm around my best friend Les…or Maddix.

Maddix, on the other hand, never shuts up. He is extremely extroverted, and the whole school is cheering him on with his baseball career. He has been playing baseball since he could walk. When Momma and Daddy realized that he has a natural talent, they decided to sign him up for select baseball. He has been playing ever since, and

2

his next step is to get a full ride scholarship to play in college. Maddix has the opportunity to get a full ride scholarship to his dream school, the University of Southern California. That is why he is practicing so much for this year's draft season. I am a little sad about it though because he will have to move out of Texas. Sometimes, I tend to feel like others compare me to Maddix. He is the "perfect" child that everyone loves. Maddix is the only one who doesn't make me feel like I have to live up to his standards. He always tells me to be myself and if people don't like me for who I am, then why keep them around?

"Maddix, Ali, hurry up! Y'all are going to be late for the last day," I hear Momma call from the kitchen. Not long after, Maddix peeks his head into my room.

"Hey, nerd, can you give me a ride? My truck is almost out of gas," he asks.

"I can't. I have to go pick up Les, but I can give you a twenty to make it to school and back home after."

"All right, that'll work. Thanks, Al. Also, don't forget I need you to throw to me after school today."

"Yeah, yeah, I know...now, go away." I hand him twenty dollars, and he skips along to leave for school. I head out not long after him. My phone is covered in texts from Les asking if I'm on my way yet. Following is a text asking if Maddix is also riding with us.

Les has been my best friend since we were in preschool. Our moms grew up together and enrolled us in the same school, hoping we would bond. I can't remember a time in my life when I didn't have Les around. I don't want there to be a time. Les is around five foot five and has long blonde hair—same as I do—and beautiful blue eyes. We have been on the same competitive cheer squad since we were toddlers. For the past three years, we have also been cheering on the Sharks at our high school, and this coming senior year, we will be leading the squad. Les will be the head, and I will be assistant head of the squad. Les has always been more athletic than me, but I am academically smarter than she is. She has also been in love with Maddix since we were in second grade but refuses to admit it. I know Maddix has a thing for her too. I don't understand why they don't just admit it to each other.

I arrive at Les's and honk the horn twice. Quickly, her front door swings open, and she skips down the sidewalk.

"Ali Grace! We are going to be late! I hope you are aware of that," Les nags.

"Well, if you would hurry up and get your license, I wouldn't have to drive you, and you could be early."

"Now, where is the fun in that, but since we are already late, let's go get some breakfast tacos. I am starving. It's the last day anyway, so what's the rush?" I look over toward her and smile. Without saying a word, she knows I agree. We head to our favorite taco stand and order four large tacos—one for me, Les, Maddix, and Jay. Then we head on to school.

"Did you read the group chat last night?" Les asks me with her mouth full of eggs and tortilla.

"No. I went to sleep early, and I also saw that it was Sasha typing and figured she was bad-mouthing Jay. I want no part in hearing what she has to say about him. He is an amazing guy who can do better." Les giggles at this comment because she knows it is true.

"So Sasha heard from Sarah that Jay cheated on her with Jessica, but Sasha thinks that Sarah made it up to break them up. However, Sasha says she is not giving up Jay that easily because she loves him and won't go down without a fight. I told her that Jay wouldn't do something like that, but Sarah kept nagging about it so now Sasha isn't talking to him."

"Les, Jay is not a cheater! Trust me. That man can barely balance school and work. There is no way he balances two girls at once."

Sasha and Sarah are my other two friends, but all they care about are the two B's and that's booze and boys. They are self-centered and only talk about what is going on in their life. Sometimes, I question why Les and I put up with them, but then I remember the free booze. On the other hand, I have known Jay for as long as I've known Les. Jay is my brother Maddix's best friend, and I always hang out with them. They are my big brothers, and nothing could break us apart...until Sasha started coming around. When Jay and Sasha first met, Sasha was sleeping over, and Jay came to hang out with Maddix. Since then, Sasha has been obsessed with Jay, which can be annoying at times because she doesn't like when Jay and I hang out. So now, Jay and I don't talk as much, but it's okay because I still have Maddix. Maddix and I do everything together. Whether it's running errands for Momma or going to parties, we are together.

"What are you doing after school?" Les asks as we pull into the parking lot.

"Les, you know Maddix needs my help practicing for baseball season," I explain.

"Ali Grace, you two need to chill. He is the best baseball player in Green Grove, and everyone knows he will do amazing!" Les sighs.

I shrug at her, and she hops out of the car in slight annoyance. I smile at her, and she laughs it off.

"Ali Grace, you are lucky I love you," she tells me.

"Yeah, I love you too, Les," I tell her as I rush to her side with my backpack barely on my back. She drapes her arm around my shoulder, and we waltz into the school as if we have been there the entire time. We sneak down the quiet hallway and peek into Jay's classroom window. He meets our eyes, and we wave him down. He raises his hand, and we hear him ask to use the restroom. After the teacher nods her head, he quickly jumps up and heads our way.

"What do you two want?" Jay smiles as he walks out of the classroom.

"Trouble as usual," I joke with him. He shoots me a smile and then points to the bag.

"Al, you know better than to bring drugs to school."

"Very funny. It is actually a breakfast taco we brought you," I inform him.

"I swear you two are the best! Did you get one for Maddix?" he asks.

"Of course. If I didn't, he would be so upset," I tease him. Then Les hands Jay the bag with both of the tacos, and he goes back to class. Les and I slowly make our way to second period. The school day takes forever. It is like a never-ending stream of misery. Les and I have every class together per usual. We slowly get through each class period. Half of them we sleep through. The other half we spend on our phones or in the restroom. We are jealous of the boys because since they are seniors, they only have to attend half the day, and it isn't fair. Shouldn't everyone be released early on the last day? After what seems like an eternity, the final bell rings. We take my car to the park, where the boys are waiting for us.

When we arrive at the park, we can spot Jay's truck from a mile away. So we park next to it and roll down the window.

"We seem to be a little lost," Les teases them.

"Oh, I think you're in the right place, beautiful!" Maddix responds to her, throwing in a wink at the end.

"Ewe, get a room, you two," I say through gagging noises. We all laugh, and then Les and I jump into the back of Jay's truck. As soon as we get in, the boys throw drinks at us.

"So it's that kind of night! Bet!" Les announces. We open our drinks and chug them. Jay starts up his truck and heads to our backroad.

We ride around, with the wind brushing through our hair. The radio is blasting on high, and alcohol is running through our blood. However, the moment is ruined by one phone call. Sasha tells Jay he has to come over, and as usual, Jay listens to exactly what Sasha says. He makes his way back to the park and drops us off but agrees to drop Les off at home on his way to Sasha's. Maddix and I play a quick game of rock-paper-scissors to see who will drive my car.

"Ha! I win! Have fun driving, loser," I say, throwing the keys at him and taking my well-earned place in the passenger seat. As we drive, drunken thoughts swirl through my brain.

"Maddix, do you ever wonder if these will be the days we look back on and wish we could have done it different?" I ask him when we get in the car.

"Al, I think that we are living life how we feel fit for this moment in time. I don't think things will get better, but they won't get worse. Girl, you just have to learn to see the positive in the worst situations," he tells me and then drives off into the pitch-black night.

Then suddenly, I feel Maddix's arm across my chest, followed by my car slowly starting to tilt.

"Maddix!" I scream at the top of my lungs as we begin to roll off the road, only to be stopped by a tree. I try to open my eyes, but they are swollen shut. I feel as if a brick had landed on my leg, but I am not sure because the adrenaline is taking control. I reach to grab hold of Maddix's arm, and I can feel it snapped in half. My stomach churns, and I try to call out again, but darkness takes over.

Sirens. Voices. Lights. Screaming. I can see the face of my surgeon, and she tries to assure me everything will be all right. But all I can think of is my brother. Did he make it?

Chapter 2

After six hours of surgery, they finally allow me to see my family. I still don't know the entire story of what happened, but I do know that we were hit. I knew deep down we shouldn't have driven after we had been drinking. Gosh, if I had just called someone, none of this would've happened. At least, we are all right, but it is a long road to recovery. That is for sure. The nurse lists off my injuries, starting with glass shards in the face, a major concussion, and, to top it all off, a shattered tibia and fibula in my left leg.

"Ali, we regret to inform you that you may never cheer again. With your injuries, it is almost impossible to return to a sport that involves so much movement and impact," the nurse tells me. I stare at her with tears welling up in my eyes. I don't believe a word she tells me because she doesn't know me. I have to cheer. It is my only escape from reality.

"Where is my brother? I want to see Maddix. I need to talk to Maddix. You are wrong about cheer. Just wait. My brother will tell you I am tougher than the rest. Where is he?" I respond to her. The nurse looks at her clipboard and writes a few notes and then simply responds with, "You need to get some rest."

I stare at her with blank eyes.

"Nurse, where is my brother?" I am asking more aggressively this time.

He has to be okay, and he made it. I mean, he is bruised and beaten also, but he is alive. Maddix survived. I know he did. We have made it through everything together, so I know we both made it.

Why won't she just answer my question? It isn't that hard to just tell me what room he is in.

The door to my room opens, and my mom steps into the room. She runs to me, embracing me in her arms. Not far behind her is my dad, and he follows her exact movements. Tears are streaming down their faces, and I can tell that they are not only crying because of me. I grab my mom's hand and look her in the eyes.

"Momma, where is Maddix? Is he okay? I want to see him, Momma," I tell her. Her eyes are filled with fresh tears, and I can tell that something is very wrong.

"He may not make it Ali. An eighteen-wheeler hit the driver side of the car, and he was knocked out on the spot. He was still breathing when the paramedics arrived. He is still in surgery, but there is little chance of survival," my mom informs me. I drop her hands from mine and am in shock.

He can't leave me. He won't leave me. He is only eighteen. He still has his whole life ahead of him. Maddix hasn't even been accepted into a college yet. Heck, he hasn't even had graduation.

"That isn't true. Where is he? That is my brother. You cannot keep me from seeing him!" I insist they let me see him. I have to see for myself. I start to pull off the wires they have attached to me. If they won't tell me where he is, then I will find him myself. However, two of the nurses hold me back while my parents try to calm me. I finally fall back on the bed, feeling as if someone just ripped away my heart, and I am the one dead. My dad holds me in his arms.

"Daddy, I need to see him. He is my best friend. I don't want to be an only child." But my dad does not respond. He just holds me, stroking my hair until I am calm. Shortly after, Jay and Les rush into my room. As soon as Les makes eye contact with me, she is by my side. She takes me from my dad, and I sob into her chest. Les sobs along with me while Jay talks to my parents about an update on Maddix. He starts to look around the room slowly, and he eventually rests his eyes on Les and me cuddled together on the bed.

"I need to take a walk," Jay says and is gone just as fast as he was here. A nurse comes in and tells my family that visiting hours are over. I am not released from the hospital until Monday, so they can do some more tests to make sure everything is all right, but they make my family leave, no matter how much I beg them to let them stay. In the blink of an eye, I am alone yet again.

*****

It is dark, and I can't see anything around me. I can feel myself sinking, but I'm not sure in what. I am freezing cold and naked. I feel myself sinking lower and lower. I try to scream for someone, but my voice is silenced. A light starts to appear out of nowhere, and I squint to see who or what it is. It is a tall figure slowly walking toward me. I am stuck, and I can't escape. No one is around to help me. I am alone.

*****

I wake up breathing extremely hard. Tears are streaming from my eyes.

"Maddix!" I scream, but he doesn't come. For the first time in my life, Maddix doesn't come to my side to calm me. No one comes—not my parents or the nurse. No one. I feel like crying again, but the tears don't come. My chest is heavy, and my heart is pounding. I can't make it without my brother. I won't make it without him.

Morning comes slowly, and I can hear the birds singing a sad song. I was hoping everything from the previous night was a dream, but reality comes rushing in when the nurses enter my room. I don't speak to them or even bother looking at them. I don't care what they tell me. Maddix will survive because he wouldn't dare leave me.

The next few days blur together like the slowest movie I have ever watched. It's the same routine each day. The nurses come in three times during the night to check on me and help me use the restroom. Then they bring me breakfast, give me medicine, and my parents come to visit for a bit. On Sunday, Les and Jay even come to see me for a bit. I tell Les that the nurse said I would never be able to cheer again, but she doesn't give me a response. Instead, she just hugs me. They don't stay long after that because they have to be home for dinner. It's finally my last night in this hellhole, but I still don't have any update on Maddix.

On the ride home, I try to prepare myself for how different life is going to be. I am on crutches for the next six months, and cheer is officially off the table. No one talks the entire ride home, and I keep my eyes closed for most of it. I can't stand being in a vehicle anymore because it reminds me of Maddix.

As soon as we get home, I sit on the couch while Daddy brings in my things from the hospital. Momma asks if I need anything, but I just shake my head. As I lie there, I stare into space feeling as if every ounce of joy has been sucked out of my body. A few hours go by, and I don't move an inch. My mom tries to get me to eat, but I'm not hungry. Eventually, Daddy comes and sits at my feet.

"Baby girl, I know it's hard, but you can't quit eating," he explains while returning a piece of my hair to its rightful place.

"Daddy, is Maddix even alive? No one has told me anything in days. How would it make you feel if your brother was in an accident and you didn't have any update for days?" I don't look at him because I know it will make my heart ache to see the pain in his eyes. It is the same pain I hold within my own eyes.

"Maddix is in a coma, and the doctors aren't sure he will ever come out of it. We are doing everything we can to keep him alive because he is a fighter, Ali. And you are, too, sweet girl. Maddix would be so mad at you if he knew that you weren't eating because of him. Ali, I know it is hard, but we cannot stop living life because of this. We have to be strong for Maddix."

My dad hands me my plate of food after he finishes his statement. I don't move at first, but eventually, I find the strength deep down inside of me to sit up. My painful eyes move from my dad to the plate. I slowly down the food, and a smile appears on my dad's face. He is right, and I have to admit that. If Maddix is going to continue to fight, then I have to continue to fight—not only fight for him, but I will fight with him.

*****

There are trees surrounding me. As I look down the path, I see someone standing there. It's a little boy. He slowly lifts his finger and points to me.

"You," he says.

"You killed me," he starts walking toward me. I turn and run, but I cannot find a way out. I turn to the left and then to the right. There are trees everywhere and no light. It is pitch black. I can't see anything. All of a sudden, I trip over a stick. When I turn around, the little boy is standing over me. He reaches for me.

*****

I am suddenly shaken awake, and my eyes shoot open. My mother is standing over me, with a fake smile plastered across her face.

"Hey, sweetie, you have a doctor's appointment," she tells me while she takes a seat next to me. I lie my head in her lap, and she strokes my hair. I used to love when my mom would play with my hair as a kid. She would be sitting on the couch watching TV, and I would crawl into her lap and set her hand on my head to hint to her that I wanted her to rub my head. Every time, I would fall asleep on her lap and wake up in my bed. I've always wondered how I would magically end up there.

"Go get dressed and meet me in the car in ten minutes," she says. I slowly get up and go get dressed. By the time I am finished, Mom is already in the car with the engine running. When we arrive, Mom drops me off at the door while she parks the car. I find a seat near the window and plop down.

"Hey, how's your day going?" I hear a sweet voice next to me ask. I look over my shoulder to see a young girl. She has short black hair and looks around fifteen.

"I mean fine, I guess. Why do you ask?"

"You just seem a little down in the dumps," she tells me. I stare back at her thinking she was joking, but she has the most serious expression on her face.

"Yeah, I haven't had the best few days," I tell her with a sarcastic laugh.

"Well, what happened?"

"You are real nosy, aren't you?" I tell her. It feels as though she is trying to solve me like a puzzle. The way she studies my every move and isn't letting me escape from this conversation.

"My brother and I were in a wreck last Friday, and he is now in a coma." After I tell her, she stares back at me. But her eyes don't look regretful or even painful. She looks at me with passion. Her look holds comfort.

"I will for sure keep you in my prayers. Umm, what's your name again?"

"My name is Ali, and you don't have to pray for me. Trust me, it won't work anyway," I tell her. She gives me a smile, but it isn't a friendly smile. It is more of her way of telling me, challenge accepted.

"Misty, my name is Misty, and it is a pleasure to meet you, Ali," she says as she lifts her hand holding the same smile. I shake her hand, and it doesn't feel like a greeting. Our handshake feels as if we just closed a bet. I don't know where this girl came from, but I do know this is not the last time I will see Misty.

During my appointment, the doctors tell me that my leg is healing exactly the way it should and that I'll be out of my cast in no time. They also say that every test they ran came back clear and that I was really lucky to be alive. I want to tell them that I don't feel lucky. I want to scream at them that it should have been me and not Maddix. But instead, I just nod at them and let my mom do all the talking. For the entire appointment, I am barely listening. I can't focus on what the doctors are telling me because I keep thinking about Misty's words.

"I will pray for you."

I have never had anyone my age tell me that. I only show up to church to humor my parents, much less pray. Who is this girl, and where did she come from? More importantly, when will I see her again?

Chapter 3

The ceremony doesn't start for another thirty minutes, but Mom insisted we show up early to help set up. The school is hosting a prayer service for Maddix at the baseball field. They announced it on the school webpage, and everyone has seen it. I hate the idea of all these people coming to pray for my brother. They don't know him. They just know of him. The only thing these people know about my brother is that he is the star baseball player and has a high chance of going pro.

Soon after we arrive, Jay and Les pull up together. I make my way to them, and we exchange hugs. People from all over town slowly trickle in. The mayor is even here, and I doubt he has ever talked to Maddix a day in his life. Even though I am slightly annoyed by the overdone prayer service, I must admit it is beautiful. The stars are beaming in the sky, and everyone is holding a candle saying prayers for him to make it. It is a little reassuring to know so many people care about him enough to stop their days to come and pray for him. However, I know the prayers don't really go anywhere, but it is slightly calming to think for a split second that they might work.

After the prayer is over, Principal Hart makes a few announcements.

"Maddix is a strong young man who is going to overcome this challenge. He is not only one of the best athletes I know, but he is the most kindhearted child I have ever met. We can all agree that this accident has been a travesty, not just for the community, but even more for his family. With that being said, the board has decided to extend the date of graduation to the middle of July, in hopes that

Maddix will be able to attend. If he is still not well then, he will receive the same treatment as every other student on a later date. Thank you for attending tonight, and everyone, please drive home safely." And with that, everyone begins to leave. A few people come hug my parents and inform them that they will continue to pray. Later, my mom finally says I can leave with Jay and Les. I leave as soon as she says the words.

On the way to Jay's, we swing by Sasha's to pick up Sarah and her. Sasha and Sarah don't know Maddix as well and don't care to get to know him. They are the type of girls who will post on their socials and caption it, "Missing you so much" when they have never even spoken to the person.

"Hey. What has all of you looking so gloomy?" Sasha questions as she hops into the passenger seat.

"Sash, we told you that Maddix's prayer service was tonight," Les shoots at her. I wasn't offended by Sasha's comment mainly because I expected it to happen. On the other hand, it does make my mood change, and I wanna lie in my bed.

"Hey, Jay, if Maddix is the valedictorian, then who is going to make his speech if he still isn't better? Sorry, Ali Grace. I hope he does get better, but what if he doesn't?" Les questions while laying a hand on my leg for reassurance.

"I have no clue, Les. Let's just pray he is here because I don't know if I will survive graduation without my man, you know? We have been through everything together, and the thought of graduating without him, I don't even want to imagine it."

You can hear the pain in Jay's voice as he speaks, and it makes my heart cry. Maddix is so important to a lot of different individuals. He has to survive. He just has to.

After we all ride around for a few hours, Jay drops Les and me off at my house. I try to reassure Les that I will be all right, but she refuses to listen to me. We get inside, and Les tells my parents hello and then grabs a handful of snacks and runs to my room. We throw on pajamas and turn on Taylor Swift. I can't remember the last time we have had a girl's night together. We do our nails and wear face masks. I want to enjoy this time I have with Les, but it is so hard to have fun with Maddix in his condition.

"Ali Grace, talk to me. I know you are upset, Boo." Les looks at me concerned while she pries. I want to tell Les everything, but I can't.

"Nothing's wrong, Les. I'm just extremely tired," I say as I crawl into my bed. Les walks over and turns the light off, and we both roll over for the night.

Chapter 4

═══════════

"Go home, Ali, he doesn't want to see you."
"Yes, he does. He is my brother."

"So now you want to see him? It has been a month, and this is the first time you are going to visit. Just go home."

"I'm almost there anyway, and he needs me right now."

"Why would he need you? You are the reason he is in the hospital. You are the reason he lost his scholarship. You are the reason he may never walk again. It is your fault he is in critical condition."

"Get out of my head! I'm not listening to you. I need to see him!"

*****

I slowly make my way to the front desk. This is the first time I have come to visit Maddix. My parents are already in the room with him, and they don't know I have come to visit. My body feels like it is going to shut down probably because I haven't had a meal in a week, and my eyes are already filling up with water.

"Room 209," the front desk lady tells me. I don't respond. I just head down the hall. What if he still isn't awake? What if he is awake and doesn't want to see me? What if he hates me and knows his accident is my fault? I have to face him and put on a brave face no matter what I walk into. I look at the room numbers, and it feels like the hallway goes on forever. The rooms pass me by one by one, and I feel like they are observing me instead of the other way around. Room 205, 206, 207, and I stop at 208. The door to room 209 is open, and I can hear voices talking. I recognize my mom's voice, and I'm assuming the unknown voice belongs to the doctor.

"We have gotten the results back from the test, and he still is not responding. We are going to continue to keep him hooked up to the machine until you and your husband advise otherwise. In my opinion, ma'am, I think it is best to say your goodbyes," the doctor informs my mother. I can't hold back, and I barge into the room. Completely ignoring my parents, I rush to Maddix's side.

"Maddix, wake up please! I know you can hear me! Quit pranking us! It isn't funny. Come home please! Just come home!" I scream at him and grab him by his arms. I try to shake him awake, but the doctor forces me to release my brother. My crutches slip from under me, and I fall to the ground sobbing. My dad rushes to me and pulls me into him.

"He isn't leaving us, Daddy. He won't do that to me. He knows I need him."

"Baby girl, we are not giving up. We will continue to run tests as long as he is breathing. He is a fighter, and we will do everything it takes to keep him here with us," my dad tells me as he helps me off the ground and leads me out of the room.

"Why don't we go get something to eat? I haven't eaten a good meal in days, and I know you haven't either." My dad starts to lead me to the exit. I want to turn around and go to my brother, but my feet keep moving with my dad, and it is as if I have lost all control of my body. We make our way to the car. I feel as if my body and mind are at war. One, two, three. My legs move forward, obeying my dad. Three, two, one. My mind is left behind, still with Maddix. However, we aren't in the hospital room. We are instead in a field, throwing a baseball and laughing as if nothing ever went wrong.

Dad holds open the door for me as we walk into Sweet Temptations. It is a local candy shop owned by Les's mom, but they also sell the best sandwiches. We walk to a booth and take our seats. Dad doesn't need the menu because he gets the same meal every time we come here. I don't touch the menu because I am not hungry in the slightest. Les comes to our table to take our order. Dad tells her his usual and then gets up to go to the restroom. Les looks at me, and I shake my head to indicate I'm not hungry. After she hangs up the order, she comes back and slips into the spot where my dad was sitting.

"Talk to me, Ali. I know that you have a lot going on, but I'm your best friend. I'm here for you, girl. You know that," Les tells me. I understand that she wants me to confide in her, and I know that I can, but I won't. I won't put all of my baggage onto her when she already has enough going on. Les is taking Maddix's coma harder than she will admit, but I'm not an idiot.

"Les, I don't want to talk about it, okay? When I am ready, I will come to you, but for now, can we just leave it alone?" I ask her.

"Of course, Ali, just know I am here," she tells me and then gets up to continue working. Dad comes back from the restroom, and soon after he returns, Les brings the food. Even though I told her I didn't want anything, she brought me my favorite Italian sandwich. I gave her an annoyed look, only to receive a smile from her, followed by a quick wink before she walks away. I guess I am hungry because I eat every bite of my food and even finish what is left of my dad's. After we finish, Dad pays the bill and we leave.

Chapter 5

Even though I constantly tell Les I don't want to go out, she insists I need to get my mind off things. I even try to use the fact that I'm on crutches as an excuse, but she doesn't want to hear it. I'm only going for the numbing feeling that comes from being intoxicated, but Les doesn't have to know that. Les and I used to go out every weekend with Maddix and Jay, but since the accident, I have no desire to go out, especially now, with everything going on with Maddix.

On the other hand, Les is very insistent on keeping things as normal as possible, with this being the summer of senior year and all. Les and I have been planning the summer of senior year since we first stepped foot into the high school building. We have this long list of crazy things that our parents would never approve, but Les can be very persuasive at times. She convinced all our parents that this was a once-in-a-lifetime thing, and they could just pretend that they have no idea what is going on. Les finalized their decision when she said they can ground us all after the summer. Sasha, Sarah, and I were not too happy about that at first, but eventually, Les calmed us down and assured us that it was a great idea. Les should really be a lawyer because she has a way with words.

"Ali Grace, what do you think of this top?" Les always asks me what I think, but she knows she looks good. She always looks good, and she has an impressive body.

"You know you always look amazing," I reassure her.

"Yeah, but do we like the pink, or should we do a more subtle color?"

"Why go subtle when you can be extra?"

"Great point. Thanks, Boo."

Les always likes to be the life of the party. She wears the cutest outfits and hangs out with the hottest guys, but for some reason, she only wants my brother. I normally just stand by her and get drunk.

"What are you going to wear?" Les asks me this every time we go out, and every time, she ends up changing my entire outfit. Here's the thing. I am not entirely fit, but I am not fat either. I don't have abs like Les, but I don't have flabs either. I always end up wearing one of Les's tops, and they always show more than I would like. I just don't argue and put the top on because Les always wins the argument in the end anyway.

"I will probably just wear what I have on Les." I know my words aren't going to slide, but I want to at least try. Maybe one day it will work.

"Umm, no. As your best friend, I cannot let you go out like that."

"Then what should I wear, girl? Nothing fits right because of this stupid cast and these crutches."

"I'm so glad you asked," Les exclaims. Then she rushes to her closet and pulls out a bright blue top that looks like it could be a bra. It crosses over in the front where my nonexistent boobs would sit and cuts off right at the hips. In the back, it ties around the neck and shows the entire back.

"Les, I am not wearing that."

"OMG, girl! Quit being a drama queen and put it on. You will look amazing."

Of course, she thought I would look amazing. I mean, she dressed me like her. After I get dressed, I look in the mirror.

*****

"You look fat."

"I know I do. Should I just change?"

"No. Les will hate you forever, and then you will really have no one."

21

"Yeah, but I don't feel comfortable."

"Deal with it. This isn't about you. Not everything is about you."

"I know, but shouldn't I only wear things that make me feel good?"

"No, wear what your friend says to wear."

"I look like a hoe. I can't do it."

"That is the only way you will get a guy to notice you. Quit being a baby and suck it up."

"Fine."

*****

I'm leaning over the sink, bracing myself on the counter with tears streaming from my eyes. I hear Les knock at the door, and I don't respond right away. I stare at my reflection. I can't let Les see me like this. She knocks at the door again, and I'm hesitant to answer, but I wipe my eyes and open the door. Les is standing there, smiling so big. However, as soon as she sees my tear-stained eyes, her smile quickly fades. She doesn't say a word. She just holds me. I feel the tears start to burn my eyes, and I don't want to ruin the night, so I pull out of her embrace and go back into her room. Sarah and Sasha are sitting on her bed. Sarah has a full bottle while Sasha has two beers—one she is drinking, and the other she throws at me after I sit on the bed and free my hands.

"You look like you have already had one hell of a night," Sasha tells me.

"Better start pregaming now if we are going to make it through this party," Les tells me again.

"Why are we going to Ty Russel's party?" Sarah complains.

"Girl, because that man is hot, and we haven't gone out in a while," Les explains. I pop open the beer and take a sip while the girls sit in anticipation.

"Feel better now?" Sarah asks.

"Let's go party!" I respond holding my drink in the air while doing a little shimmy with my shoulders. The girls holler and join in on my little boogie. I smile for the first time in a while. I genuinely smile. My friends are pretty great, and I couldn't ask for better. Next thing I know, I see Les running at me with a pillow. She shows no mercy, and neither do the other two.

"Girls, my drink. Watch the drink!" I scream. They giggle as I surrender.

"She really was more worried about her drink than her broken leg." Sarah laughs as she helps me up after the attack is over. I shoot her a little smile before sitting at Les's vanity.

Les helps me touch up my makeup before we leave while Sarah and Sasha fight over the front seat. Even though they both should know Les is going to get the front per usual.

Chapter 6

On our way to the party, Les had all the windows down, blaring some Taylor Swift. Thing 1 and 2 are in the back, sticking their heads out the window like crazy dogs. Maddix would get such a kick out of them. Sometimes, I wish life was as simple and easy as they make it look…just sticking your head out the window and not having a care in the world. They always tend to keep things interesting.

"Are you kidding me right now?" Sasha screams.

Oh no, here we go. We almost made it to the party. Here's the thing. Every time we go out, Jay and Sasha are fighting. It doesn't matter when or where, they are in a fight.

"What happened this time?" Les questions because she already knows what Sasha was screaming about. This happens every time without fail. Sometimes, we are lucky if we can get halfway through the party before they start fighting. I guess we aren't so lucky tonight.

"Jay just told me that he is sitting with the boys and to text him when I get there so I can come to find him," Sasha tells us. I look at Les, and she is already smiling. Stupid. The reasons are always so stupid. I try not to laugh because Sasha always gets so agitated when Les and I laugh, but we can't help it. She is so sensitive, and I have no clue how he puts up with her. Les finally notices I'm looking at her, and she just giggles and shrugs.

"Girls! I'm serious! Quit laughing. I can't believe he won't come find me. He is really going to make me come to him. He is so annoying," Sasha complains.

Les just turns up the music, and Sarah takes away Sasha's phone. She reminds her that this is going to be a fun night. We finally get to Ty's house, and it is packed. We expected that though because we always arrive late. We all strut up to the house, except for me because I can barely walk, and all eyes are on our group because, obviously, we are the girl group everyone wants to be a part of. Sasha refuses to go find Jay, even though Sarah has given Sasha her phone back by now. However, not long after we get to the house, Jay starts walking over to our group.

"Let's go. I need a beer pong partner," Sasha says as she grabs Les's hand.

"Oh my gosh, what's her deal now?" Jay asks me. I just look at him and smile as I chug the rest of my drink.

"What? Did I do something?" I just shrug and start to follow my friends, leaving Jay standing there alone.

"Ali, you are so freaking annoying," he calls after me. I turn around and blow him a big kiss. Then I hop on one of the guy's tailgates to watch. He asks me if I want a beer, and of course, I say yes. I like parties a lot better when Maddix is around because we will sit on the bed of his truck drinking and making fun of people who are falling down drunk. My favorite time was when Maddix was talking to this one girl named Jessica. He brought her to a party with Jay and me. Well, let's just say she had a lot to drink and ended up in the pool. The look on Maddix's face was priceless, and they didn't last long after that. He has always told me how he wants a nice and genuine girl, and not someone who is constantly partying and only wants "one thing." He wants genuine love, like the kind you find in the movies. I think Les and him should just admit they like each other, but they refuse.

I grab another beer and hop off the bed of the truck to walk around so I can clear my head. The guy next to me tries to assist me, but I don't let him. Just because I only have one functioning leg doesn't mean I can't take care of myself. As much as I would've loved to sit there all night, if Maddix knew I was sitting around sulking at a party, he would make fun of me. So for his sake, I go talk to our friends. Most people I speak to ask the exact same thing…

"How are you doing?" I wish I could scream at them that I'm hanging on by a thread and wish it was me and not Maddix. Instead, I just grab another beer.

After talking to people for a bit, I see a familiar face mixed into a crowd of girls.

"Misty?" I ask, and she turns around. Standing right in front of me is that strange little girl from my appointment.

"Oh, hey, Ali, what are you doing here?" She asks me.

"Honestly, I have no clue, but shouldn't I be asking you that question? Aren't you like fifteen? You shouldn't be at a party like this, and you definitely shouldn't be drinking," I tell her. She gives me a warm smile before replying.

"Ali, I'm here with my older friends, and I'm not drinking because I am sixteen and will be driving all my friends home tonight. I don't want to be liable if anything is to happen." I can't believe she told me that. She knows that my brother was in an accident, and I was with him. Does she necessarily know that we were drinking? No, but that is beside the point.

Instead of saying anything, I turn around and get away from her as fast as I can. I grab a drink from someone and decide that I am finally drunk enough to be a pro at beer pong. Les and I partner up and go against these two guys from our class, who I must say are superhot, but we didn't do good at all. While Les and I are laughing, I feel a hand slide around my waist. I turn to see Ty Russel standing there with a huge grin on his face. He just stood there holding my waist, so I continued playing the game. He honestly was making it easier to balance. I've never had a boy touch me in any way actually. With Maddix always around, they are all intimidated. I guess since he is gone for now, they are feeling really brave.

I have had boyfriends in the past, but Maddix always scared them to death, so they never wanted to do anything more than kiss. Most of them were too scared to even cuddle with me because they thought Maddix would walk in and get pissed. But Maddix isn't here, and I am free to do whatever at this moment. Before I know it, the alcohol takes over. I turn around and kiss Ty hard on the lips. Ty kisses me back and rubs his hands down my back. We stand there making out in front of everyone until Les lets out a cheer. It startles me, and I pull away. Ty and I stand there holding eye contact for what feels like forever.

I grab the device from his hand and inhale. It is my first time ever vaping, but I figure that if all the cool kids do it, then it isn't that bad. The fuzzy feeling that overcomes me quickly makes me regret my decision, but I refuse to let it show. I turn around and continue my turn at beer pong. While I'm playing the game, Ty is kissing my neck and holding me by my waist. I am starting to get annoyed and keep pushing him off. He persistently comes back laughing and telling me to quit playing. His hands start to wander, and he tries to lower his hand down my body. Ty ignores my resisting and just tries to pull me into him again. I quickly realize I messed up. What am I going to do? Ty is tall and strong, and I stand no chance.

"Ty, stop please," I say calmly. I don't want to upset him, but he starts to get aggressive.

Then he leans down into my ear and whispers, "Ali, you started something that you have to finish." With that, he aggressively picks me up and carries me toward the house. I am terrified. I know I cannot let him get me in there, but I am too intoxicated to do anything. I try to scream for help, but nothing comes out. What have I done? Ty seemed so sweet. I never would have thought he could do something like this. I just want to explore my newfound freedom, but I never dreamed it would go this far.

"Hey, bro, where do you think you're taking her?" A voice comes from behind us. My head jolts around, and I lock eyes with Jay. Yes! Jay, my hero, is coming to save me. Ty tries to come up with a lie, but he is too drunk for it to make any sense. Jay finally gets tired of the nonsense and goes to grab me from Ty's arms to take me away. I happily brace myself on Jay while waiting for Les to arrive. I can see her from a distance coming to rescue me with my crutches.

"Jay, Jay, Jay. You are so silly if you think Ali is going with you. She got herself into this mess, and if she doesn't want it, she would say something. Now leave me and this hoe be. We have business to tend to." He laughs.

"Oh hell, no," Jay yells. Before I could say a word, Ty was on the ground, and Jay was on top of him. He was hitting him repeatedly—left, right, left, and right. With every swing, Jay hits him harder. To add to the chaos, Sasha lets out a blood-curdling scream.

"Jay, you're going to kill him!" she yells. Some of the other football boys try to pull Jay off, but he just keeps going. I just sit there watching, wondering if I should video or break up the fight. But before I could make a decision, we heard loud sirens coming from a distance.

"Cops!" Someone warns. Everyone starts ditching. There are people jumping fences and hopping into their vehicles to drive away. Jay runs to pick me up, but before he does, I hit Ty with my crutch while he is still down.

"Don't ever touch me again you overweight hippo!" I scream.

I hear Jay burst out laughing behind me, but he doesn't have time to praise me. He picks me up and throws me over his shoulder like a sack of potatoes. We run outside, and he takes me to a bush where we crouch down and hide until the cops leave. Maddix would love all this commotion!

Chapter 7

"He's dying."

"I know he is. I know he's dying."

"You need to go see him right now. Get out of bed."

"I can't. I can't see him. They won't let me."

"What if he dies tonight and you never get to see him again?"

"There is nothing I can do! Shut up!"

"Ali, you aren't going to get to say goodbye. He is going to leave you all alone."

"When will you leave me alone?"

"Never, Ali. I am you."

*****

As I open my eyes, the sun sets them aflame. My head feels like someone just filled it with helium. There is no memory from last night, and it scares me. What happened? How did I get home? I reach for my phone on my nightstand, and it is nearly dead. I also have a million texts from my group chat. Hopefully, this can tell me what happened.

> Sasha: Did everyone make it home safe?
>
> Sarah: Yeah. Is Ty okay? Jay beat the crap out of him!
>
> Sasha: I don't know, and I also don't know where Jay is. I haven't heard from him since the cops showed up.

SARAH: He probably went with Ali to make sure she got home safe.

LES: Well, I'm happy Jay stopped Ty before he could hurt Ali.

SASHA: Les, there was no reason for Jay to fight Ty. Ali was going with him willingly.

LES: Sasha WTH! No, she wasn't. Ali was drunk and couldn't do anything about it. Plus, she can't walk, and Ty was carrying her. That's why I went to tell Jay.

SARAH: Les, you told Jay? It's your fault Ty is in the hospital?

SASHA: Wait. Ty is in the hospital? Who told you that?

SARAH: I'm texting Ty's sister right now. She said he has a broken jaw and nose.

LES: That prick deserves it for whatever he was going to do to Ali.

SASHA: Look, I love Ali, but again, she wasn't resisting, so I think it was unnecessary. Even if she is on crutches, she wasn't fighting against him when he picked her up.

LES: Sasha, she is also going through a lot with her family right now. Either way, Ty shouldn't have tried anything, knowing all the things going on with Maddix.

SARAH: She has a point, Sash. Maddix means everything to Ali, so she is vulnerable right now, and Ty took advantage of that. Also, I can't blame her for not fighting against him. He would've hurt her if she did. She was drunk and scared.

SASHA: Well, it's not Jay's job to babysit, and now, he is probably going to get charges pressed against him.

LES: Jay is Maddix's best friend, so while he isn't
around, you know Jay is going to protect Ali
at all cost.

SASHA: Ugh, that is so stupid. Ali is a big girl and
doesn't need my boyfriend to take care of her.

SARAH: Sasha, you know Ali is in this group chat.
She is going to read all this crap so shut up.

SASHA: Well, she should because Jay is mine.

LES: Sasha, sometimes you really need to shut up!

After I read this, I decide I have better things to do than deal
with Sasha. As I slowly make my way to the kitchen to get some
water, I decide to text Jay to make sure he got home safe. But when I
walk into the living room, there is someone on my couch. I can't see
who it is, but I am not taking any chances. I balance on one foot and
use my crutch to sneak up on the figure. I rip back the blanket and
start hitting it with the crutch. As I'm beating the figure, it lets out a
girly scream, but I know that scream, and it isn't a girl.

"Jay! What the heck! You scared me!" I yell at him and hit him
with the crutch one more time just as payback.

"Why are you yelling at me? You're the one who just beat the
crap out of me with a freaking crutch! How are you even standing?"

"Well, you're the one who is sleeping on my couch without me
knowing," I argue.

"I wanted to make sure Ty didn't try to get into your house and
do something."

"Jay, I can handle myself. Your girlfriend said so in the group
chat," I say as I enter the kitchen to get some Tylenol and water.

"Oh, really? Because you didn't look like you were handling
yourself very well last night. Also, I will handle Sasha. Don't worry
about her. She is overdramatic at times." I don't remember anything
from last night. That comment sends shivers down my spine.

"Jay, what happened last night? I read the group chat, but I'm
still confused. Why did you beat up Ty? What was he trying to do?"

"Ali, Ty almost took advantage of you last night. I went after
him, and then the cops showed up so I threw you over my shoulder

and we ran. Then, after they left, I drove you home and helped you get to bed. You insisted on showering though, and I didn't want you to drown because, well, you know," he says gesturing at my leg.

"So I helped you. But I swear nothing happened, and I didn't see much. I kept the curtain closed and just checked on you here and there to make sure you didn't die. Then I helped you get dressed and laid you in your bed. After that, I decided to stay on the couch so I could make sure Ty didn't try anything else."

My words are caught in my throat, and I stare at him in admiration. He is such an amazing person, and I don't deserve him as a friend. Any other guy would've tried to sleep with me, but not Jay. I wonder why. I always wonder why Jay is so sweet to me, and he jeopardizes his relationship every time he hangs out with me. But before I can say anything, Jay gets a call. I already know who it is before he tells me.

He steps outside, and all I can hear is yelling. Gosh, I hate when people yell. It brings back terrible memories. My parents used to fight all the time, especially over bills and their work schedule. Dad would say Mom needs to work more, but Mom would argue that one of them has to be around to take care of Maddix and me. Maddix has always been so good at lightening the mood. If they were fighting, he would simply make a joke or he would cook dinner to surprise them. If it was a really bad fight, he would sneak into my room, and we would watch movies and play games. Once, we snuck out to the park and met up with Les and Jay. We were intoxicated while we played at the playground. This was my sophomore year, but toward the end of the year, our parents hardly ever fought. Maddix and I would go to parties and practice baseball for his future career, and everything was perfect.

Jay came back inside and told me he had to leave. Apparently, Sasha was freaking out about last night, and when he told her he was at my house, she said he had thirty minutes to get to her house, or they were over. After he left, I turned off every light in the house and went to sleep. I want to forget everything Jay told me.

*****

Trees are all around me. They are taller and wider this time. The path is more narrow. At the end of the path stands three figures. They all point to me and smile.

"Your turn to suffer," they all say in unison. I turn to run, but I am blocked by trees. They are surrounding me, and I cannot escape. The figures come closer and closer, repeating the same thing.

"Your turn to suffer. Your turn to suffer." They taunt me.

I cover my ears screaming, but there is no noise. No one comes, and I am trapped by them. I cry, but there are no tears. I try to cover my ears, and it does not help. I rock back and forth. Back and forth.

*****

I jolt up in my bed, unable to breathe. This dream has been haunting me for weeks. The attacks get worse as the dream gets more visible. I keep screwing up in everything I do. How do I change the outcome? I reach for the little device under my pillow. I close my eyes, and I feel the deadly toxin slowly make its way into my lungs. My head feels as if clouds have submerged it. I hold it in there, hoping it will just end the pain. The toxin will endure my suffering. It's okay though because I deserve it. I'm a terrible friend and an even worse sister.

I didn't sleep much the rest of the night. I stayed up. I wasn't crying, and I wasn't thinking. I was just vaping. Ever since that night at the party, I will do whatever it takes to erase those memories. The thought of his lips makes my stomach churn. What made him think that was okay? There is so much going on in my life, and now this. I have never felt more vulnerable. I should've screamed and fought him. I don't know why I didn't. What was I thinking letting him kiss me? I should've known it wouldn't have been enough for Ty Russel. He is greedy. I'm happy Jay was there because that jerk got what he deserved!

Chapter 8

I wake up to my phone ringing. I look at it, and I have twenty missed calls from Les. I jolt awake, and realization hits me like a bullet to the temple. Today is the first cheer practice, and we are late. Even though I can't walk, I still am going to cheer practice so that when I am done with recovery, I know the routine.

I dress as quickly as I can and drive to Les's, speeding the entire way. I can't believe I've made us late for the first practice of the new season. I pull into Les's driveway and honk the horn twice. As usual, Les comes running out two seconds after. She jumps in the car, and I quickly pull out and get to the gym as fast as my car will let me.

"Ali Grace, slow down! We are already going to be late because somebody couldn't wake up on time," Les tells me.

"Sorry if cheer isn't my number one concern right now. You know, being as how Maddix is in the hospital, and I can't even participate," I shoot back at her sarcastically.

"Well, Ali, life has to keep going on whether we like it or not." Those words left me speechless.

"Les, how can you do that?"

"Do what?" Les asks as if oblivious to the situation at hand.

"Act like everything is okay. Les, it's not. Maddix is dying, and it is my fault!" I just blurted it out. I didn't mean to, but it just came out.

"Ali, it isn't your fault. Maddix is dying because he was in a crash."

"You don't know anything. It is my fault, and now, I may lose him forever."

"I get it, it sucks. Trust me, I get it."

"No, you don't Les. You don't get it because your family is perfect. Geez!"

Les just looks at me and scoffs.

"Please tell me you are joking, Ali. Yes, Maddix is your brother, but you are not the only one being affected in this situation. I have been in love with him since the day I met him, and now, I may never get to tell him. Do you know how it feels to be in love with someone and then lose any opportunity to be with them. The audacity you have to look me in my eyes and say I don't understand."

In all honesty, I couldn't even believe what I had just said. Why would I say such a thing? Les is a great friend and is just trying to help me.

"Les I—"

"No, I get it Ali," she cuts me off. The rest of the drive, she did not speak to me.

We arrive at cheer practice, and Coach gives us a disappointed look. Les starts to explain, but she doesn't want to hear it. Les runs over to the rest of the girls, and I make my way to the stage. I plop up on the side and let my feet dangle over the edge. I sit there watching the other girls learning the routine. I attempt to follow along, but without a working leg, it is almost impossible.

During water break, I am sitting alone because Les still won't speak to me. I am looking around for her, but I can't see her. That is when I spot a group of girls pointing at me and laughing. My heart immediately drops to my stomach. How dare they talk about me like I'm not sitting right here. Tears begin to sting my eyes, but I can't let them see me cry. If I cry in front of them, they will only make fun of me even more. I hop off the stage and grab my crutches. I walk out of the gym easily because no one tries to stop me. I have decided I am never coming to another cheer practice again.

Practice finally ends after what feels like an eternity. The team comes flooding out of the gym, and I spot Les talking to some of the girls. About halfway down the steps, she meets my eyes. Then she turns to the group of girls, says something to them, and then runs over to my driver's side window.

"So I'm just going to get a ride with Sasha. You can call me when your attitude changes," Les tells me before I can roll down the window completely and is gone before I can speak.

After the fight last week at cheer, I stubbornly decide to stay home from today's practice. However, I am so sick of sitting in my room. Instead, I make a big pitcher of sweet tea, grab a book, and go sit on the porch. Not long after I get comfortable, I see someone coming down the road. I squint my eyes and notice that it is Misty walking down the road. I try to avoid eye contact, but she still notices it's me and doesn't hesitate to walk right up the porch steps and sit down next to me.

"How are you feeling?" She asks me. At first, I don't want to acknowledge her presence, but I know deep down she isn't leaving until I respond.

"Honestly, Misty, I feel like my entire life is caving in on me. My best friend won't talk to me, and my brother is dying because of me. Oh, yeah, and I haven't seen my parents in days, and I don't know what is going to give out first—my lungs or my liver, but I hope it happens soon because I can't take this anymore!" I didn't mean to spill out my heart to Misty, but for some reason, I felt like I could trust her. Maybe it was the fact that when we first met, she didn't judge me. There is something different about her.

Misty doesn't meet my eyes. Instead, she holds her gaze on the sky. I look at her, not only in question but in awe.

"Do you ever sit and look at the sky and wonder if God is listening to your conversation?" Misty says softly.

I am taken aback by her comment. I am not religious. I don't believe that God cares about my life. If He does, then why are bad things constantly happening?

"Misty, I don't believe in God. If He exists, then why do all these bad things happen? How could a God, who is supposedly good, let all these horrible things happen?" I ask her.

"Ali, you know that God exists because how can you be so angry with someone who you don't believe in? It is simply not possible. He does love you, Ali, and He will always love you. You just have to let Him love you." And with that, Misty simply gets up and continues her walk down the road, leaving me sitting on my porch contemplating what she told me. What does she mean by let Him love me? Also, if He had any love for me, He wouldn't be letting my brother die. Misty doesn't know what she is talking about.

After sitting here on the steps for a while, I head to my room to sit in the dark. When I walk through the door, I see Maddix's old teddy lying on my floor. I pick it up while heading to my bed and lie down cuddling it. I used to steal it from him all the time because it is big and fluffy. Maddix would get annoyed, but he never would take it away. He wouldn't cry about it either. He would grab a different teddy and try to play a game with me. I always laughed at the funny voices he would make. On my ninth birthday, he decided he was too big for the teddy and gave him to me. I was so excited that I wouldn't have to share it with him anymore. He may have gifted it to me on my birthday, but we both knew I claimed that teddy a long time ago.

While I am lying in my bed killing my lungs, my door abruptly swings open. My mom is standing dead still in my doorway. Her face is fuming with anger.

"Ali Grace! Why did I get a call from your cheer coach saying you missed practice today and walked out last week?" My mom questions. I quickly hide my device under my pillow, hoping she didn't see it.

"I don't know," I lie.

"Don't you lie to me, Ali! You know that it is a sin to lie to your mother." I roll my eyes. Of course, she brings that up. My mom was raised in a Catholic family. The words Misty told me have been on my mind all day, and now, my mother brings it up. Fine. I do believe there is a God, but I don't think He loves me. After everything I've done, how could He? I don't live a good life. I am a sinner. My mother, on the other hand, is perfect, of course. She believes in His love. I know God loves my mother, but He will never love me.

"I know it is! Trust me, you tell me every time I sin. Well, you know what, I don't care. God put Maddix in the hospital. He lets us have financial problems. God doesn't love me, and even if He did, I don't want His love. He is killing Maddix, and I can never forgive Him for it," I scream at her.

She stares at me blankly, and I can tell she doesn't know what to say. I have never spoken to her like that. I always hide my opinions and wake up every Sunday to go to church with no complaints.

"Who are you? You are not the daughter I have raised. The Ali I know would never speak to me in such a way."

"The Ali you know is a fake! You don't know me. You are barely home and never spend time with me. Wanna know something, Mother? I wish it were me who was dying. Actually, I wish I would've died on the spot! Then I wouldn't have to deal with this family anymore. Maddix has always been the favorite golden child. But me? I'm just the disappointment. I bet you wish it were me in the hospital also so that your precious Maddix could live out his dreams." I spit the words out and immediately regret everything I just said. Covering my mouth, I can see tears swelling up in my mother's eyes.

"Mom, I…I didn't mean—" I stutter.

"No, Ali. I'm a terrible mother. I just clothe and feed you. I pay for a roof over your head, and you never wonder where your next meal comes from. I pay for your cheerleading. Everything you have ever asked me to do, I find a way for you to participate. You know why, Ali? It isn't because I'm selfish. It is because since you were born, I have wanted nothing more than for you to achieve everything you love in life, but I see now it has all been a waste of my time. I'm done trying with you, Ali. Now, do whatever you want! I am going to take care of my golden child."

"Mom, I am suffering from anxiety, and you can't take five seconds to see that. I wake up every night scared out of my mind, and I never know why. I get so mad at the littlest things, and I can't even figure out why I am so upset. Do you know what that is like, Mother? To feel scared dusk till dawn and never know why?"

"Ali, quit being dramatic! For once in your life, think of someone else besides yourself. You are not suffering from anxiety. You are a hormonal teenager who wants attention. Maddix is dying, and you can't stand the fact that everyone is giving him their full attention," she says the words calmly, but it feels like she just shot me in the heart.

My own mother called me a liar. I finally build up the courage to tell her, and she calls me a liar. Tears burn my eyes, and I can't even look at her. Instead, I grab my jacket and push past her making my way toward the front door. I can hear her calling after me, but I ignore her.

Chapter 9

I don't know where I'm going, but I keep running. I feel the slow sensation of pain flowing up my body. I don't stop running. I feel the wind running its fingers through my hair as if to brush it out. I don't stop running. Puddles cover the road, and I don't dodge them. I feel as though if I stop, I will fall right through them into a different world, where people live forever, mothers never judge, and friends are friends forever. You can never be alone. I keep running straight, but nothing is familiar. The more I run, the scarier it becomes. I quickly glance behind me, and I see it. It is chasing me, so I speed up. However, my feet then get stuck, and I cannot move. The trees start to grow from the ground and create a cage surrounding me. Voices scream like nails on a chalkboard from all directions. I try to cover my ears, but my hands refuse to move. Birds start to dive at me and pierce my skin. I attempt to dodge them, but nothing works. My mind and body are disconnected and refuse to listen to each other.

"Let me go!" I scream. Then it ascends from the shadows. I know the figure, the shadow standing in front of me.

"Who are you? What do you want from me?" I demand. The shadow lifts a grungy finger toward me and whispers.

"Your life." After the statement, the wind picks up, and I fall into darkness.

*****

My eyes are wide open now, and I sit up. My lungs refuse to work, and I am trembling. My eyes examine where I am. My hand makes its way to the grass so I can brace myself. It is not long before I calm down and realize I am in the backyard. My crutches lie next to me in the grass. Tears begin to sting my eyes. I hope every time that I close my eyes and wake up, this won't be my reality, but every time they open, I am still in a cast, and Maddix is still gone.

"What else? What else are you going to put me through? Aren't you supposed to love and protect me? You are tearing my world apart! You have taken everything from me! I haven't done anything, and I have never done anything to you, so why are you punishing me? Why are you ruining my life?" I scream up at the sky, with rivers of tears running down my face. My entire body trembles, not only from the wind outside, but with fear. I clench the grass with all my might, gasping for air between sobs and clenching at my heart.

"This isn't fair! You have taken everything! My hopes and dreams, my family, my friends…you have even taken my dignity! What else do you want from me?" I roar out into the world. I can't take this anymore.

After calming down a little, I make my way over to the swings. They have always been mine and Maddix's favorite. Every time Mom would take us to the park, we would race to the swings. We would make bets on who could swing higher. Then after months of begging our parents, they finally bought us our own swing set.

"If I swing higher than you, then you have to give me your candy bar," he would tease me. We both knew he could swing higher, but he always pretended he couldn't. Mom would prepare our lunch while Dad would push me since I was at a disadvantage being younger.

As I'm sitting on the swing in the dark, I feel someone coming up behind me. A bad sensation comes over me, and I attempt to get up, ready to run. Before I can, a familiar voice calls out to me.

"Now, why are you sitting here in the dark sulking by yourself? I know I raised my princess to be stronger than this." I turn around, and before his face is even in full view, I throw my arms around his neck, and he wraps his arms around me to keep me from falling.

"Daddy," I sob into his chest. He doesn't say a word and just holds me. I'm assuming Mom told him about our fight. After a few minutes pass by, I calm down, and we sit on the swings together. We don't look at each other, and we don't speak. We sit in silence, enjoying one another's presence.

"What's going on with you, Squirrel?" Dad asks after a while.

"I don't know Daddy. I don't even know who I am anymore," I inform him.

"Squirrel, it is normal to be confused. You are a teenage girl, but no matter what, you have to respect your mother."

"I know, but she called me a liar. I'm not a liar. I am struggling also, and it feels like you two have forgotten about me. I am still here, Daddy. I am still breathing. I miss Maddix with all my heart, but you two act as if I don't exist." I have always found it easy to talk to my dad. We are practically the same person.

"You remember that time when you convinced me to wear your princess tiara while I pushed you because it gave me powers to make you swing higher? Maddix made fun of me the entire time, but I didn't care because it put the biggest smile on your face," my dad says.

"You told me that as long as I was happy, you didn't care what anyone said," I remind him. He still lives by that to date. Dad is one of the strongest people I have ever met. He provides for our family and still manages to make it to most of our events. My dad has been through so much in his life, but he never lets it show. He is the type of person that will give you the shirt off his back if you don't have one. I know when I get married one day that my husband needs to be exactly like my father. He treats me like I am his princess. When I fall down, he picks me up. When I cry, he wipes away my tears. When I am mad, he makes me laugh. But ever since the accident with Maddix I don't see him much anymore, or when I do, he is too stressed to talk. He doesn't seem like himself anymore, but as usual, he isn't going to let me know.

"Let's get inside, Squirrel. We have a delicious dinner waiting for us."

He holds his hand out, and I grab it. I love my dad. He always knows exactly what to say.

When we get inside, I can smell freshly cooked pancakes from the back door. Mom isn't home anymore. I'm assuming she went back to the hospital. Dad asks me if I want to watch a movie, but I tell him I'm too tired. I grab a few pancakes and head to my room. I'm not actually tired, but the numb sensation has faded, and my clouds left my head. Once I lie down, I immediately allow smoke to take over my lungs while I watch my show. Of course, I'm not going to eat the pancakes, but I don't want Dad to get suspicious.

Later that evening, my door swings open. I know that I'm caught when I see my dad staring at me with a blank expression. Smoke fills my room, and I can see tears welling up in his eyes.

"Ali Grace," Dad says, his voice breaking. He rarely calls me by my full name. My heart drops, and I wish I could take it all back. I wish I would have never started smoking. I wish I would've never gone to Ty's party. I wish I could take back everything I said to Les. Most of all, I wish I hadn't drunk that night so I could've driven us home safely.

"Why? What did I do? Why would you stab me in the back like this? I do so much for you. I am always on your side in every situation. Why?" The disappointment in my dad's voice makes me want to disappear. I don't answer. I'm not even sure what to say. How do I look my hero in the eyes and tell him I don't want to be alive? What do I say to make him understand I wish it were me in that hospital bed?

"Ali Grace, say something! You cannot ignore me!"

"I need to go," I say simply. I try to push past him, but he grabs my arm and pulls me back into my room.

"You cannot keep running away from your problems. You will stay in your room until I decide what to do with you. I can't believe you would do this to me." And with that being said, he shuts the door.

I wait for thirty minutes before throwing my crutches out the window and sliding down the drainpipe. That house is too suffocating, and I need to escape. I can't take the car because they will hear the engine start and then I'll really be in hot water. So instead, I hobble down the block.

As I walk, I look up into the big sky full of dazzling stars. While staring at the sky, I remember a poem Maddix would tell me when I

43

was younger. When Mom and Dad would fight, we would sneak out the window and lie under the stars. When the fighting would echo, he would repeat the same few lines.

> One sun apart
> I'll always come back to you
> Eight planets to separate us
> But I'll always come back to you
> Millions of stars create a wall between you and I
> But I'll always find my way to you
> Billions of galaxies pulling us in
> But you'll always be my home

I can feel the tears dripping down my face. I can't imagine my life without Maddix. He is my best friend. Not many people understand our relationship because it is very unusual for a brother and sister to love each other as much as we do. But every time I go to the store or just walk down the street by myself, people would always ask where my partner in crime was. They don't do that anymore though because they know exactly where he is. He is lying on a hospital bed, fighting to survive.

I walk three blocks and end up at Jay's house. I go around to the back of his house and jump the fence. He is sitting in his backyard, playing with his dog Cooper.

"Hey, Ali, what are you doing here? Did you walk all the way here? You know better than to be using your crutches that much. It isn't good for your arms," Jay says. I turn around, and Cooper immediately runs to me, jumping on my legs.

"I needed to escape from my house, and I know what times your parents aren't home," I inform him. I lie next to Jay on the ground, and Cooper runs to my lap. Jay makes a sad face, and I giggle as I pet Cooper. He has always loved me more than anyone. None of us are sure why he is so fond of me, but I'm not complaining.

"Have you heard any updates on Maddix?" Jay questions as I grab the cigarette from him and inhale deeply.

I don't look up at him. Instead, I continue petting Cooper, hoping that the question will disappear, but it doesn't.

"No, my parents aren't really talking to me these days," I eventually say.

"Dang, what happened?"

"Mom found out I've been skipping practice, and Dad caught me smoking in my room."

"Oh, Ali! You, okay?" Jay asks while fidgeting with the grass below his feet. Tears begin to flood my eyes, and my words are tied in a knot. A slight stream escapes my eyes, but Cooper licks it away, whimpering at the sight of me being sad. Jay is now staring at me, waiting for a response I'm not sure I'm going to give. He puts his arm around me and pulls me to his chest, not asking any more questions. I rarely cry, so when I do, he knows things are bad. We lie back in the grass, and while I am lying on his chest, I can feel his heart racing. I wonder why he is nervous. Jay and I hug all the time. Why is this time any different?

"Sasha broke up with me. She said that I was self-centered, and she knew I was cheating, which isn't true. I'm not sad though. I was going to end things soon anyway because I am sick of the drama," Jay tells me. I have to admit I am surprised when he tells me. Jay was head over heels for Sasha when they first met, but I guess things are never as good as they may seem. But I already knew that seeing as everyone on the outside looking in thinks my family is perfect. In actuality, we are all slowly breaking.

"Honestly, Jay, you deserve so much better than her. She has never treated you right, and you know that," I told him while staring into his deep blue eyes. Jay turned away pretty quickly though. He has never enjoyed holding eye contact with people. He always says it makes him feel way too awkward.

"Trust me. I know. She was constantly on me about cheating, and I understand she has trust issues, but come on, man. If I was going to cheat, I would've done it months ago. Trust me. You know how hard it was to stay loyal sometimes, Ali, especially when I'm alone with you," Jay tells me, and I jerk my head up to look at him, but he is still looking at the ground.

"Do you know who Misty is?" I ask him, attempting to change the subject. I don't know what Jay meant by what he said, but I do know, I am not ready to know.

"Who?" Jay asks.

"Misty. She goes to our school and is at all the parties. Dude, she lives on our block," I explain to him, but the look on his face tells me he still doesn't know who I'm talking about.

"Well, she is weird and is always trying to talk to me about God. She tells me things like He loves me and dumb crap like that." After I make that comment, Jay's head pops up and stares at me.

"Ali, you do know I'm Catholic, right? I believe all of that. I don't understand why you wouldn't." As the words come out of his mouth, his eyes don't look judgmental. They look comforting, but they also aren't the color of Jay's eyes. Jay has blue eyes, but in this moment, his eyes are a dark brown.

"I need to go," I tell him, quickly standing up. I don't understand what I just saw. That wasn't Jay, but it was Jay. This doesn't make any sense.

"Well, let me at least walk you home, Ali. I didn't mean to upset you, and it's real late. You don't need to walk by yourself," Jay tells me, standing up and dusting off his pants, which are covered in dirt. I keep my eyes on the ground. I do not want to meet his eyes. I am ashamed to meet Jay's eyes but not because it's Jay. What is going on with me? There is no way that it was a trick of the light. I mean, his eyes are a sky blue, and they were a comforting deep brown! I am going insane.

We have passed a few blocks, and Jay hasn't said a word to me. He is walking by my side in silence, staring up at the stars. There are so many questions I have, but I'm scared to say a word. What he told me before is heavy on my mind. I keep replaying what he said about me in my head. "Especially when I'm around?" What does that mean? I don't know how I am going to react, but I know one thing—I need answers.

"Hey, Jay, what did you mean earlier when we were sitting in the yard?" I question him. He hesitates for a moment. I can't see his face, but I know the look that takes refuge there.

"Just forget about it, Ali. It was nothing," he responds.

Nothing? How can he say that? There is no way he hasn't been stressing all night also. How can he expect me to just forget those words? Men are so confusing. I can't stand them sometimes.

We continue walking, and I don't say another word. Jay keeps stealing glances at me but thinks I don't notice. I want to scream at him for getting into my head. I am in such a weak state and already have so much on my mind, and now, he throws this into the mix. The least he could do is explain to me what he meant. But before I know it, we are walking up my driveway. I hesitate to go inside, still wanting an answer, but after what feels like an eternity, I start to walk away. I feel Jay gently grab my arm before I am out of reach to stop me from leaving.

"Ali…" He speaks so softly I can barely hear him, but he is unable to disguise the longing in his voice. It is right in this moment I know my answer. I don't turn around. Instead, I shrug his hand off my arm and continue my journey into the war zone that I once called home.

Chapter 10

Standing in the mirror, all I can see is a stranger staring back at me. She looks like she has her life together...beautiful blonde hair and a smile painted on her face. But the mirror is only holding a lie. She is broken, and there is no fixing the girl in the mirror. The girl who used to stare back at me is gone, and the girl who stares back now will be gone soon.

"Ali, let's go. We are going to be late," My mom yells from the kitchen.

"I'm coming," I tell her and head to the kitchen.

"I don't understand why we have to attend this stupid graduation if Maddix can't even be there," I inform my parents.

"Ali, you do not get a say in anything we do. We don't trust you to make smart decisions. So you will go with us whenever we leave the house. Jay is graduating today also, and we would like to see one son walk across the stage, so get in the car now." I have never heard my mother so upset before.

We arrive at the graduation, and there is an extreme amount of tension when people begin to notice our presence. The entire time that we scan the stands looking for Jay's parents up until the point when we sit down, you could've heard a pin drop. It is almost as if someone hits play as soon as we take our seats. As soon as we sit, the ceremony begins. One by one, the graduates walk out and have their picture taken. Slowly, the line grows smaller, and I find myself holding my breath in hopes that Maddix will appear in the lineup.

"Margey Justice, Alexander Knewman, Jay Warren..." The announcer says all these names over the intercom as they walk out.

After he announces Jay, everyone around me begins to roar with excitement. Everyone except me because I know that is not what he wants. Jay is going through the motions right now and doesn't want to be here. Who could blame him? He has to graduate without his best friend. How is that fair? Everyone else in the class gets to graduate with their best friends, but not Jay.

"Is anyone sitting here?" I don't need to turn my head to know who is asking. She is always here at the worst moments. Doesn't she know how hard this is on us?

"No, Misty, that seat is empty, but I don't think you want to sit there because you will be associated with the family whose son can't attend," I tell her, hoping it will scare her away.

"Nonsense! I will be sitting by my friend to enjoy watching these students take the next step in their lives." As she is saying this, she is taking a seat right next to me. When she sits, her shoulder brushes against mine and a rush of calmness floods over my body. I no longer feel mad or anxious. Instead, I am calm, and I enjoy the rest of the graduation.

After they give out all the diplomas, it is time for the valedictorian speech. I think that they will skip over it, seeing as how their valedictorian is currently unable to give his speech, but I am proven wrong when I hear a voice begin to speak.

"I never thought I would ever make it to this day, much less give this speech. I am obviously not even close to worthy of stepping in for Maddix, but Principal Hart asked me to give a speech in his place. I sat at my computer for days, wondering what I should write. That's when it hit me that Maddix already wrote his speech." Jays voice floods through the stadium, and it is as if everyone has stopped breathing. I am fuming with anger that they decided to continue with the speech. This is supposed to be Maddix's moment, and they have taken that from him also. I want to walk up there and drag Jay off that stage. Nothing about this is fair to Maddix.

"Trust in the Lord with all your heart. Never rely on what you think you know. Remember the Lord in everything you do, and he will show you the right way (Proverbs 3:5–6). This Bible verse reminds me of the world's most annoying puzzle—the Rubik's cube," Jay continues as he picks up a small square full of random colors.

"So today, for my speech, I've decided to show everyone how to solve this puzzle, not using what I know, but by letting God guide me. Our education at Green Grove High School is a lot like a Rubik's cube. I think of our school with three layers. The first layer is spiritual. It's not something you can learn in a day. It takes a bit to understand everything, but once you do, it all clears up a bit." The entire time he speaks, he is turning the cube left and right. He finally holds it up for us to see, and one side is solved. Jay brings the cube down and begins to move the cube around between his fingers as he continues speaking.

"You're not done yet though! Which brings me to the second layer of our school—the friendships. In Green Grove, we have small classes. By having that, we all become closer friends. This is an experience that many kids don't get in their schools. These friendships and experiences are something I will never forget. I will carry with me this unique privilege, and a very unique one it was with a class full of creativity. Of course, we had our differences, but in the end, we were all the best of friends, and this concludes the second layer of our cube." Jay holds the cube up to the sky again, and another side is solved. The entire stands are focused on Jay and the speech. I must admit I am even slightly invested.

"Now we're getting close to solving this complex puzzle, just one step left. In my opinion, this is the hardest layer. You get nervous, even scared, that you'll mess up everything you've worked so hard on. This layer is the academic layer. Now, the academics at GHS aren't easy. You have to study, bring your stuff to class, do your homework, and turn in all of your work on time. It can get confusing at times. You mix up the assignments or forget that you have a test the next day, but in the end, it all works out all right." Again, Jay holds up the cube, and another side is solved. Every time Jay begins speaking, it is as if everyone stops breathing. Then as soon as he lifts up the cube, a giant wind overcomes the stands.

"Then, it is time to prepare for college. You sign up for scholarships and take the SAT or ACT. These steps are a vital step into college, and they just so happened to have solved our puzzle!" Jay proclaims, and the entire crowd begins to cheer. I must admit a small cheer escapes from my lips because I didn't even think he would accomplish the puzzle. Then Jay starts to mess with the puzzle again, and everyone quiets down to hear what he will say next.

"So I would like to conclude this speech by saying farewell to Green Grove and hello to adulthood." Jay holds up the puzzle for a final time, and it is a mixture of colors yet again. Everyone begins to stand up and cheer as Jay leaves the stage. I'm not surprised with how good Maddix's speech is. He has always been good with words, and while I'm still annoyed, at least everyone got to hear what he had to say.

The rest of the graduation goes by, and before I can blink, it is over. Maddix has officially missed his own graduation. Nothing about this is fair!

Chapter 11

I get up to get water in the middle of the night, and I overhear my parents talking again about taking Maddix off life support and letting him go. I barge into their room, screaming at them for giving up. They are quitters and have given up on their own son. They try to explain that there is no hope, and it is the best choice for him, but I know better. Maddix wouldn't give up on me.

After I leave their room, I end up here, staring at a person I used to know. I want to escape this picture that I've painted for myself. I fling open the medicine cabinet and grab the bottle of pills and go into my room. I lock my door and sit on the edge of my bed, pouring the bottle of pills into my hand. I hold death in my hands, and I know this is the only way to end the pain. I've lost everything! What is the point of carrying on another day? I lift the pills closer to my mouth and take my last deep breath. But before I can take them, I feel a warm hand grab my wrist.

"Ali, don't do it." But when I look up, I see no one. I shake my head, assuming I am hearing things due to lack of sleep. I continue with my decision and raise the pills back to my mouth.

"My child, this is not the only way. I love you," someone tells me, and I can feel arms around my body. I sit here for a few minutes before turning to see who it is, but again, no one is around. Instead of feeling scared, I feel safe. This isn't the voice I normally hear. What is going on?

I return the pills to their container and put them back into the medicine cabinet. I don't know what I was hearing, but there has to be a reason I heard it.

I am lying in my bed, covered by a cloud of smoke when I hear my window open. I refuse to move. Instead, I slowly grab the loose board off the headboard and prepare to beat the crap out of someone. I can feel them getting closer, and I try to time my attack perfectly. But then, I hear them speak.

"Ali, I swear if you hit me with that board, then I will go get your crutch so you can see how it feels." I turn around and fall into his eyes. Jay is standing in my room, and I have never been happier to see him. But instead of running to him like I want to, I stay exactly where I have been all night.

"Why are you here, Jay? Just go home. I don't have the energy to fight with you."

"I'm not here to fight with you. I'm here because my mom told me the news, and I figured you could use a friend." Before he finishes his sentence, he makes his way toward me, and I don't stop him. Instead, I surrender myself to him, and he holds me in his arms.

"Jay, they can't give up on him. It isn't fair. He wouldn't give up on us." I sob into his chest, and he lays his chin on top of my head. I can feel his heart pounding in his chest.

*****

"Let go of him. You are only going to hurt him."

"No. I love him. I can't."

"If you love him, then you need to get rid of him. You are only going to destroy him. He doesn't need you in his life. He needs to move on and do better."

"But I can't handle losing him. I've already lost my brother. I can't lose Jay."

"Jay has enough going on though. You need to let go of him and let him live his life without you in it."

"I love him though, but I can't tell him yet. Not now. There is too much going on, but if I let him go, I will never get to tell him."

"Quit being selfish and think of someone other than yourself. Do you think he actually cares about you? He is only around because of Maddix. If it weren't for him, Jay wouldn't have a single care for you. Let go of him! Let him go!"

*****

Tears stream down my face as I hold onto Jay. I don't want to let go. It's the last thing in the world I want to do, but the voice is right. Jay deserves the world, and I can't give that to him. He also is only taking care of me because he loves Maddix and thinks he has to take care of me while he isn't here. I need to release him of his duties because he has his own life that he needs to continue living. And sadly, I cannot be a part of it anymore.

"You need to leave," I tell Jay as I push him away.

"No, Ali. I am not leaving you while you are in this state of mind," Jay tells me while reaching for my arm, but I pull myself out of his reach. As much as I want to let him hold me, I can't let him.

"Jay, I'm not your responsibility. I can take care of myself. Just leave please." I try to sound as if I am all right, but I don't want him to leave. There is nothing I want more than for him to stay. I want him to tell me how he truly feels and to feel his warm kiss against mine, but that is just a dream. My voice is right. I can't keep holding him back. As much as I want to be with him, I need to think of what he needs, not what I want.

"Jay, get out of my room please. I don't want you here. I want you to get out. Just get out!" I scream at him. But he holds his place firm. His eyes stare into mine, daring me to make him leave because he isn't going to do so willingly.

"Ali, I'm not leaving because I'm not stupid. I know you're not all right, and I also know you are not my responsibility. I am not here because I feel I have to be. I am here because I want to be. I want to be here for you, but not because you're my best friend's sister. I want to be here because I love you, Ali, okay! I finally said it. I was keeping it inside because you have so much stuff going on in your life, but I love you, and nothing you say or do will keep me from loving you," Jay tells me.

Then he makes his way over to me slowly, and I let him. I don't move or speak. I simply stare into his dreamy eyes. He is sincere and means every word he is saying. He slowly grabs my hand and holds it to his chest. I can feel his heart racing.

"This is what you do to me, Ali. Every time I'm around you, this is what my heart does. Ever since we were kids, but I never thought Maddix would approve." This comment snaps me back to reality. I pull my hand from his and move to the other side of the room.

"So since Maddix isn't here, now you have the courage to tell me? Why couldn't you tell me when he was still around? Because you knew he wouldn't approve so you waited until he was gone? Is that why you bought the alcohol? You planned the crash so that he would be gone and then you could get your chance! You really will do whatever it takes to get into my pants, won't you? Because I'm Maddix's sister, and no one ever gets with his sister, so you would get all the praise! Are you kidding me right now? I should've known you weren't genuine. You are just like every other guy!" I yell at him. I am so agitated right now. How dare he make me feel so vulnerable just to get with me.

"Ali, you know none of that is true. I am leaving for college next week and couldn't leave without telling you how I truly feel. Say the words, and I won't go. I will stay here with you." He tries to move close to me again, but I flinch with his first step. I want to believe his words and beg him to stay, but that isn't fair to him. He needs to go and live his life. Who am I to keep him from his dreams?

"Please just leave Jay. I don't want to be around you," I say to him.

"Fine, Ali, but not because I want to…only because I know you want to be alone right now." And with that, he turns to my window and leaves. As soon as the window closes, I collapse to the ground, but I am not careful, and I hit my broken leg, yelping in pain. I know getting rid of him was for the best, but I can feel my heart shattered into a million pieces. I'm not sure which hurts worse—my leg or my heart, but I know I would rather be dead than in this pain.

*****

"You might as well just end it all. Your life isn't important to anyone. You have nothing left. Maddix isn't coming back. Les wants nothing to do with you. Mom and Dad wish it were you in the accident. Jay doesn't love you. You will never cheer again. What is the point of living? Your lungs and liver are already giving out. You might as well finish the job."

"But what if Maddix comes back, and I'm not here? That won't be fair to him."

"Then cut yourself. Let the blood flow from your wrist but not to the point where is kills you. Not yet. Give yourself the pain you deserve."

Chapter 12

One cut.

Two cuts.

Then a third.

There is a knock on the bathroom door, and I quickly pull down my sleeve.

"Come on, Ali. You are going to be late for your first day of senior year," my dad informs me from the other side of the door.

"Almost ready," I respond. However, I will never be ready for today. Nothing can prepare me for today. Not seeing Jay and Maddix in the hallways. Not driving Les to school and getting our breakfast tacos. More importantly, I will never be prepared for the looks and whispers.

I got my cast off two weeks ago and have been attending physical therapy three times a week so I can get back to cheer as soon as possible. I cannot miss out my senior year, and I need to be better by college tryouts. I am now in a brace that goes from my thigh to my ankle. It is bulky and ugly. I hate wearing it, but at least, I am walking—not very well, but I am walking.

"You can't dress a little nicer for your first day?" My mom asks me when I enter the kitchen.

"Well, Mom, there isn't much I can wear with this thing on my leg," I tell her while motioning to the giant cage on my leg. Mom shrugs off my comment and proceeds to have me pose in the front yard for pictures. Once she finishes, we say our goodbyes. I head to my car as fast as I can and peel out of the driveway.

I am halfway to school when I see someone walking in that direction. I notice her right away and pull over.

"Get in, Misty. I'll give you a ride," I insist, and she doesn't refuse.

"Thank you so much, Ali. My legs are killing me." I give her a sarcastic glance.

"Oh, my bad," she giggles, and I giggle also. We drive the last mile to the school, and when we arrive, Misty turns and looks at me.

"How are you feeling about today, Ali?" Misty questions.

"Misty, it has been three months, and he still hasn't moved. I can't focus on school. Not to mention my best friend hates me, and I pushed away the one guy I've ever loved. I am confused and lost. I have no one. Also, the looks I am going to get as I walk down the hallway? Just the thought makes me want to cry. I am not strong enough, Misty. I can't do this." After I finish, Misty takes my hand in hers, and that calm feeling floods back once again.

"Ali, you have made it this far, so you might as well finish what you've started. Also, who says you have to do it alone. I will walk with you, and we can face the stares and whispers together." I nod, and we slowly make our way to the school. Misty and I stand at the entrance of the school, and before we push our way in, she grabs my hand and squeezes it to give me reassurance. I don't understand why, but I know I am going to be all right because I have Misty right beside me.

I take a deep breath, and we push open the doors together. Immediately, it is as if life is sucked out of the room, and everyone stops what they are doing in order to stare at me. I want to bow my head in shame, but when I look at Misty, her head is tilted up, with a wide smile on her face. I almost forgot we were holding hands, and that is what gives me the strength to look up and smile. If she can stand by my side and not be ashamed, then I can lift my head high and not be ashamed of who I am.

I finally make it to my locker, and that's when I notice Misty is gone. I never felt her hand leave mine. I look around to try and find her so I can thank her, but she is nowhere to be found. I spend most of the day trying to find her. In between classes, I search for her. At lunch, I try to find where she is sitting. After school, I search the school for her, but I can't find her anywhere. Thats when I realize I made it through the first day. I have been so busy wondering where Misty went that I didn't even notice all the gossiping. I have almost decided to give up looking for her, but when I get into my car, Misty is sitting in the passenger seat, almost as if she had never left that spot.

"Girl, where have you been all day?" I ask her.

"In class, at lunch, and around the school. Did you not feel me leave you this morning?" She asks me. I tell her I did, but the truth is, I felt like she was with me all day. That calm-controlled feeling that comes when she is around stayed with me the entire day.

I am lying on the couch when I hear a knock at the door. I don't feel like talking to anyone, so I ignore it. I'm assuming it is the mailman or Karen from across the street with another casserole.

"Ali Grace, I know you hear me knocking!" I freeze when I hear her voice. It can't be her. We haven't talked in weeks. Slowly, I make my way to the door, thinking of a million things I can say to her. I have replayed this conversation in my head on repeat, but now that it is about to happen, I have lost all ability to talk.

I unlatch the door and slowly open it to find Les standing there, still in her school clothes.

"What are you doing here, Les?" I ask her. She gives me a confused look and then sighs.

"Listen, Ali Grace. Today wasn't the same without you. We have been riding to school together since we started high school. First, Maddix would drive us. Then when you got your license, we started the breakfast tacos tradition. I really miss my best friend. Not to mention I had to hang out with Sasha and Sarah all day, and let me tell you, that is never fun. Can we please be all right, Ali Grace? I miss you." I stare at Les with a blank expression while she talks. It takes me a few seconds, but I finally work up the courage to speak.

"Les, you need to leave," I spit the words out so quickly I didn't even know I was speaking until she gave me a surprised look.

"What do you mean, Ali Grace?" Les asks me.

"I mean I don't want to be friends with you anymore. I don't need you, Les. I don't need anyone. I am doing great by myself. So just leave. Go be the captain of the cheer squad and the most loved girl in school. I'm good where I'm at." I try to shut the door after I finish, but Les pushes her way into the house.

"Les, I said you need to leave," I yell at her.

"I heard you, and I'm not listening. You might be able to fool everyone else, but you can't fool me. I have known you since we were in diapers, Ali Grace! You can't blind me with your lies!" I don't want to keep arguing with her, so I decide I want to leave. I turn to go out the front door, but Les realizes what I am doing and grabs my arm. As soon as she does, my shirt sleeve comes up and her eyes meet my scars. I swear everything in the world stops, and I stare at her while she stares at my wrist.

"Ali Grace, when did you start harming yourself?" Les asks me. I don't respond to her. I simply jerk my arm from her grip and run to my room. I quickly close the door and lock it, sliding down the door as tears make a river down my cheeks. I can hear Les talking on the other side of the door, but I am not listening. I don't care what she has to say because she knows I am pathetic. For the rest of my life, when she looks at me, she will see me as broken.

*****

As I sit on my bedroom floor, the ground begins to shake abruptly. I try to stand, but gravity pulls me down, and I can't move. The ground beneath me gives way, and I fall straight through my floor and hit the dirt with full force. The trees begin to grow around me.

"No! Please stop this!" I scream as loud as my voice will let me. I turn in circles, looking for an escape, but there are four of them this time...one blocking each exit. They all walk toward me, and they talk at the same time. It's only four of them, but it sounds like the entire world is screaming at me. I fall to the ground in terror, screaming. Suddenly, I feel someone hugging me. I slowly look up, and it is all gone. I am no longer in a forest, but I am sitting in a meadow.

"Ali, let Les come back into your life. She loves you and wants the best for you," the voice tells me. However, this isn't the voice I normally hear. It is different and calm.

"I can't! I will hurt her. I hurt everyone I let into my life. I am a toxin, and anyone who comes near me will parish," I argue.

"That is not true, My child. Do not fear, I am with you. Do not be anxious. I am Your God. I will strengthen you. I will help you. I will uphold you in My victorious hand."

Chapter 13

I walk into the kitchen to find my parents standing there with Les. I stop dead in my tracks, and it takes them a moment to notice I am standing there. They tell Les goodbye, and she leaves without saying a word to me.

"Hey, Squirrel. Why don't you come take a seat." My dad motions to the seat next to him. I hesitate for a second and then plop down. I can tell my mom has been crying, and I already know what this is about.

"Ali, we are extremely sorry for not believing you. We haven't been the best parents lately, but we are here for you." Dad holds me in his arms as he speaks. I am filled with relief because they finally believe me.

"Sweetie, I have contacted Father Augustine, and he has recommended the best counselor to help you. I am not a huge fan of counselors because I think you could just pray more, but if it's what you need, then we will do it."

I laugh at my mother when she tells me this. She has always told me to pray a little more and all my worries would go away. I used to think she was insane, but now I see her point.

"We are sorry that it took Les coming to us for us to believe you. You are our daughter, and we will do anything to protect you. There is no excuse for what we did." As my dad speaks, I see a little tear escape his eye.

"You have your first appointment tomorrow, so get plenty of rest, okay?" My mother tells me. I hug them both as tight as I can and then head to my room.

As soon as I get into my room, I search for my device. I smile and open my window.

"Goodbye, death. Hello, salvation!" I scream as I throw the device out of the window. It is time for a change, and that starts today.

I am sitting in the waiting room, anticipating my name being called. I have never openly shared with anyone how I am feeling—well, besides Misty and Jay. Jay—gosh, I miss him. I should've told him how I feel, and now he has probably moved on.

"Ali," the receptionist calls, and my head pops up.

"You may head back now. It is the third door on your right." I nod my head and slowly walk down the hallway. My mind goes back to the first time I went to visit Maddix, but instead of Momma and Daddy sitting there when I walk in, there is a lady.

"Hello, Ali, it's a pleasure to meet you. My name is Ashley." She gets up to shake my hand as she speaks. I grasp her hand to shake it, and there is immediate comfort.

"Now, I don't expect you to simply start talking about all of your problems to a complete stranger. Heck, I wouldn't do that either. So instead, let's play a game." After she finishes her statement, she turns around to grab the game of Jenga. I am confused on what this has to do with my problems, but she is the professional I guess.

"The game of Jenga has always been my favorite game. However, I have added a twist to it. Each piece has a question for you to answer. The yellow is easy, the green is medium, and red is hard. You get to pick whichever of the three colors and answer the question." Mrs. Ashley smiles at me as she begins to set up the colorful version of Jenga. I should have known there would be a twist. I decide to pull out the yellow one first because I don't know this lady, and she doesn't need to know all my deep dark secrets right off the bat.

"What is your favorite color, and why?" I read aloud. She gives me a look full of question. She seems genuinely curious of what my answer will be.

"Black, but not the sad black. My favorite color is the black you see when you look into the night sky and see a universe full of endless opportunity." I look up at Mrs. Ashley when I finish speaking. She is smiling as she picks a green block.

"What motivates you to keep trying? I would have to say my children and my husband. They are always reminding me to never give up because they need me." I must admit, I kind of expected Mrs. Ashley's answer, but her reasoning was not even close to what I thought she would say. I decide to pick the red next. How hard could the question really be?

"What is your biggest regret?" I suck in a breath. That is not what I was expecting.

"Take your time, Ali. That's a hard one," Mrs. Ashley reassures me. I don't want to answer, but then I remember I am here for healing.

"I wish I had decided to drive my car the night of the wreck. Maybe I would have seen the eighteen-wheeler coming and could have saved my brother. It was my car. I shouldn't have made him drive. He rarely drives my car because he has his own truck. I should've driven. That is my biggest regret, not driving my own car." When I finish, Mrs. Ashley wipes away a tear.

"Can I tell you something, Ali, or would you like to continue the game?"

"Tell me, Mrs. Ashley, what can I do to make things right?" I ask her.

"Ali, you have done nothing wrong. Yes, I understand it was your car, but neither of you two would have known that you would get into an accident. God has a plan for you, Ali, and I believe that if you look a little deeper into the situation, you will find his message," Mrs. Ashley states.

We continue for the rest of the hour, and before I know it, our time is up. I feel a sense of sorrow when she tells me it is time to leave. I honestly enjoyed getting so much off my chest. I walk into the lobby, and Momma is waiting there to pick me up.

"How was your first day?" She asks when we get into the car. I take a minute to respond because I want to find the right words. I finally settle with.

"I can't wait to go back."

As we pull into the driveway, I see Les sitting on the front porch. I look over at Momma with an annoyed look.

"Ali, just listen to what she has to say and quit being so stubborn." My mom drops me off and heads to the hospital as I slowly walk to Les. There are so many things running through my head I don't know where to start. The second Les sees me, she runs to me and throws her arms around me. I wrap my arms around her waist and begin to cry. I have missed my best friend. No, I have missed my sister. I can't believe I thought my life could ever be complete without her in it. She saw me when I was happy, and she sees me when I'm broken. Without her, I would have never gotten the help I need.

"How was your first day?" Les asks as we take a seat on the front porch.

"It was great, and it felt amazing to get everything off my chest. Les, I am so sorry that I pushed you away. You didn't deserve anything I said to you," I tell her.

"Ali, stop. You are in a place of grief, and I didn't understand. Instead, I got upset, which isn't fair to you. I should've known right away you weren't all right." After she finishes, I pull her in for another hug, and instead of crying, this time, we laugh.

"Also, Jay may have confessed his love to me before he left for college." Before I even finish my statement, Les is up on her feet.

"What? Ali, you have been in love with him for years! What did you say?" She is standing in anticipation, waiting for my response.

"I made him leave. I am not in the state where I can love someone the way they deserve, especially Jay. Not to mention Maddix would kill me if he knew I hooked up with his friend while he was gone." I tell her with a smile, but Les's face drops, and she is no longer beaming.

"About Maddix—" Les begins.

"Ali, a few weeks ago, Conner L. asked me on a date, and I had an amazing time. Then two nights ago, he asked me to be his girlfriend, and I said yes. I know everyone has had this thought that Maddix and I would end up together, but he had his chance for years, and frankly, I can't wait any longer. I am sorry, Ali. I really am."

Les stares at me with a worried look. I look back at her and begin to laugh.

"Conner? He's superhot, Les, and sweet! I am so happy for you, girl!" Then we begin to squeal like a bunch of chipmunks.

"You're not mad?" She asks me.

"Les, my brother is an idiot because he didn't ask you out years ago. It isn't your fault, and he can't expect you to wait around while he goes out with all these other girls." We sit on my front porch for what feels like hours. I explain everything to Les, and it feels amazing to finally let her know. We are in the middle of a conversation when my phone begins to buzz with a million texts. I pick it up, and my face drops instantly.

"Les, it's Maddix. I need to go." I don't wait for her to respond. I run to my car and drive to the hospital as fast as I can.

Chapter 14

I run through the hospital doors and scan the room for my parents. They are sitting in two chairs in the waiting area. Both of their eyes are stained with grief, and I know the news is not good.

"Momma, Daddy, what is going on?" I ask as I walk up to them. Momma immediately looks at my dad and begins to cry. Daddy wraps his arm around her and looks up at me. He doesn't look into my eyes but into my soul, which sends a chilling shiver down my spine.

"Ali, we have decided to take Maddix off life support. His vitals aren't changing, and the doctors say he shows no signs of life. They say he will be gone immediately after they turn the machine off because it is the only thing keeping him with us. We know how much he means to you, Ali, but you are doing better. You have Mrs. Ashley and Les now. They will help you through this. Also, we all have each other, and we will overcome this."

I look at my dad with terror as he speaks. I can't believe they are giving up on him. He would never give up on us, and he has too much to live for.

"No! I will not give up on him!" I scream as tears escape my eyes one after the other. I run from my parents and go searching for Maddix. Why can't I remember what room is his. I turn every which way in search of my brother. I will not let him go! Maddix is my best friend! He helps me up when I fall. He wipes my tears when I am breaking. He hides me from the dangers of the world, and I can't live in this world without him.

After searching for what feels like ages, I finally find his room. It is flooded with nurses and doctors. How dare they stand here and watch my brother die. They don't know him or what he means to so many individuals.

"No! Stop! I will not let you kill my brother! He is going to come back! He will! You need to give him more time!" I scream as I attempt to push through all the nurses. Finally, they all give up and let me through. I run to Maddix's side and immediately drop to my knees.

Not long after, my parents come running through the door. The nurses don't try to stop them. Instead, they let them come comfort me, but I don't need them to. I look to my right, and Misty is on her knees next to me, praying. She doesn't look up. She focuses on what she is saying. My mom makes her way to the other side of the bed and falls to her knees and begins to pray the same prayer as Misty. Then I feel my dad's hand on mine as he kneels next to me and bows his head in prayer. I am looking around at everyone I love in this room together praying to God to save my brother. Quickly, after everyone starts praying, upon the request of my parents, the machine that has kept my brother alive for months is turned off.

"What are you doing? Let him live! Do you not see how many people love him! How dare you!" Then I turn to Maddix.

"Fight, Maddix! Show them how strong you are! Show these nonbelievers that you will live! Think of your family and think of baseball! Maddix, please!" I scream at him, begging him to keep fighting. In spite of the anticipation of what the next few minutes will hold, no one around me has quit praying. They continue the same prayer, and I finally hear it, and I know this prayer. I fall to my knees, I hold my hands, and I bow my head as I begin to pray.

"Our Father, Who art in heaven, hallowed be Thy name. Thy kingdom come, Thy will be done on earth as it is in heaven," we begin. While the seconds seem like an eternity as we are praying over Maddix's lifeless body, we are too deep in prayer to realize the room is now full of nurses and doctors, staring in disbelief as Maddix takes his first deep breath on his own…without any machines! We finish our prayer while the medical team jumps into action. Maddix is alive!

Chapter 15

I visit Maddix every day for the next few weeks. He is making prog-ress every day. Doctors say it's a miracle he is breathing on his own. Every time I visit Maddix, I tell him of what I learned at my Bible study for that week.

"I am here to visit my brother, Maddix," I tell the lady at the front desk, even though she already knows. I walk down the hallway to my brother's room. However, when I turn into his room, I see him sitting there wide awake. He is not alone, though; sitting on the edge of his bed is Misty.

"Maddix! You're awake!" I say in excitement as I throw my arms around my brother.

"Hey, little sis, Misty is just catching me up on everything I've missed." I stare at him and Misty for a second.

"How do you two know each other?" I question him. No one seems to know who Misty is, and every time she is around, no one questions who she is.

"Well, that's one way to greet a friend! Maddix, I must be on my way. Have a blessed life, and I'll always be around," Misty says with a wink before exiting the room.

"Al, come sit. We have a lot to talk about." Maddix motions to where Misty was once sitting. "Al, I know Misty because I sent her to you. She was my guardian angel, but I had no need for her while I was in my coma. I sent her to watch over you and care for you while I couldn't. She is now your guardian angel and will be with you no matter where you go. She gave me this to give to you so you can always remember she is with you."

69

Maddix pulls a necklace from under his blanket. On it is guardian angel wings. I turn around so that he can clasp the necklace onto my neck. I tear up just a little because of all of this information. I almost don't believe he is telling the truth, but the more I think about it, Misty was always there at my worst moments. Anytime I was going through a tough time, she appeared out of nowhere. Misty is not only my guardian angel; she is my friend, and I love her for everything she has done—not just for me, but for Maddix.

*****

"Ali! Al help!!" I can hear Maddix screaming for me from his room. He has been home for a few weeks now, but his anxiety attacks have been more frequent due to his PTSD. I don't mind him waking me up in the middle of the night though. He has always been there for me. Now, it's my turn.

I grab a glass of water from the kitchen and go into his room. I crawl next to him in bed, and he begins to sip on his water.

"What do you hear?" I begin to ask him.

"Your voice," he responds.

"What do you taste?"

"Water."

"What do you smell?"

"Your perfume."

"What do you see?"

"You, Al, and I thank the Lord you are still here." After he says this, we sit in silence for a second before he begins to speak again.

"Ali, where is everyone? When I went into the coma, Jay and Les were with us. Now, Jay came to visit once, and I'm pretty sure Les has moved on." He looks at me with sorrow-filled eyes. He lays his head on my shoulder as I stroke his hair. I can't blame him for wondering. One day, his life was perfect, and the next day, he needs help from everyone. He used to pitch a perfect pitch, and now, he can barely walk. I look down at him and remember something I was told once.

"Do not fear, I am with you. Do not be anxious. I am your God. I will strengthen you. I will help you. I will uphold you in my victorious hand."

Chapter 16

I am sitting at my desk finishing up my next speech when a little head peaks in through the door.

"Mommy, Daddy said it's time to go, or we are going to be late for church."

"Okay, Misty. Tell him I will be in there in a second," I respond to my daughter.

I quickly submit my speech for review before my next show and walk to the kitchen. My family is standing there waiting for me.

"Ali, come on, or Misty is going to be late for choir. We need to leave now."

I grab my purse as I say, "Jay, calm down. I am coming. I had to finish what I was doing."

We get to church and sit in our usual seats next to Maddix and his wife. Misty quickly runs up to get ready for choir, and we sit quietly as we wait for church to begin. I catch Jay staring at me and give him a look. As a response, he gives me a peck on the head.

"I love you, Ali Grace," he whispers.

"I love you too, Jay." And then the piano begins to play, and the angel choir sings while both of my Mistys sing along.

About the Author

Addison is a seventeen-year-old girl who lives with her parents and four siblings. She still attends high school and is a resident of Texas. Addison was raised Catholic and plans to use her gift of writing to spread the word of God to all that are willing to read a few books. Known as Addi to her friends, she identifies strongly with Ali, the central character of her first novel. Having experienced many of the same difficulties as Ali, Addi herself has sought the light and found it. Her greatest wish is to share that light with other young adults by helping them to navigate the path to its shining.

Printed in the USA
CPSIA information can be obtained
at www.ICGtesting.com
CBHW022047180824
13252CB00044BA/409